Dear Panda

Miriam Latimer

D1586798

Essex County Council

3013020623779 3

Dedicated to the real Flo and Bea. xx

DEAR PANDA
A RED FOX BOOK 978 1 849 41654 2

Published in Great Britain by Red Fox,
an imprint of Random House Children's Publishers UK
A Random House Group Company

This Red Fox edition first published 2013

1 3 5 7 9 10 8 6 4 2

Copyright © Miriam Latimer, 2013

The right of Miriam Latimer to be identified as the author and illustrator
of this work has been asserted in accordance with the Copyright, Designs and Patents Act 1988.

All rights reserved. No part of this publication may be reproduced, stored in a retrieval system,
or transmitted in any form or by any means, electronic, mechanical, photocopying, recording or otherwise,
without the prior permission of the publishers.

Red Fox Books are published by Random House Children's Publishers UK
61–63 Uxbridge Road, London W5 5SA

www.randomhousechildrens.co.uk
www.randomhouse.co.uk

Addresses for companies within The Random House Group Limited can be found at:
www.randomhouse.co.uk/offices.htm

THE RANDOM HOUSE GROUP Limited Reg. No. 954009

A CIP catalogue record for this book is available from the British Library.

Printed in China

The Random House Group Limited supports the Forest Stewardship Council® (FSC®), the leading
international forest-certification organisation. Our books carrying the FSC label are printed on FSC®-certified paper.
FSC is the only forest-certification scheme supported by the leading environmental organisations, including Greenpeace.
Our paper procurement policy can be found at www.randomhouse.co.uk/environment

MIX
Paper from
responsible sources
FSC
www.fsc.org   FSC® C104723

Florence had just moved house. She liked her new room, and her new garden, and most of all, Florence liked that her new house was right next to a zoo.

Florence loved seeing all the animals, but the one she liked best was the panda.

But even pandas couldn't make Florence feel better when she got a letter from her new school.

Florence Perkins
Zoo Road
Bamboory
Devon

Dear Florence,

We're looking forward to seeing you on the first day of school. We'd love you to stand up in front of the whole class and tell us all about yourself. You can tell us about your favourite food, your favourite game, and any special friends you have.

Yours sincerely,

<u>Miss Brook</u>, Bamboory School

Florence didn't want to stand up in front
of all those new people, and what's more,
she felt sad that her friends were a
long way away, back at her old school.

"What if I don't make any new friends?"
she thought.

But then Florence had a brilliant idea!

She ran to get some paper
and a pencil and she started
to write a letter.

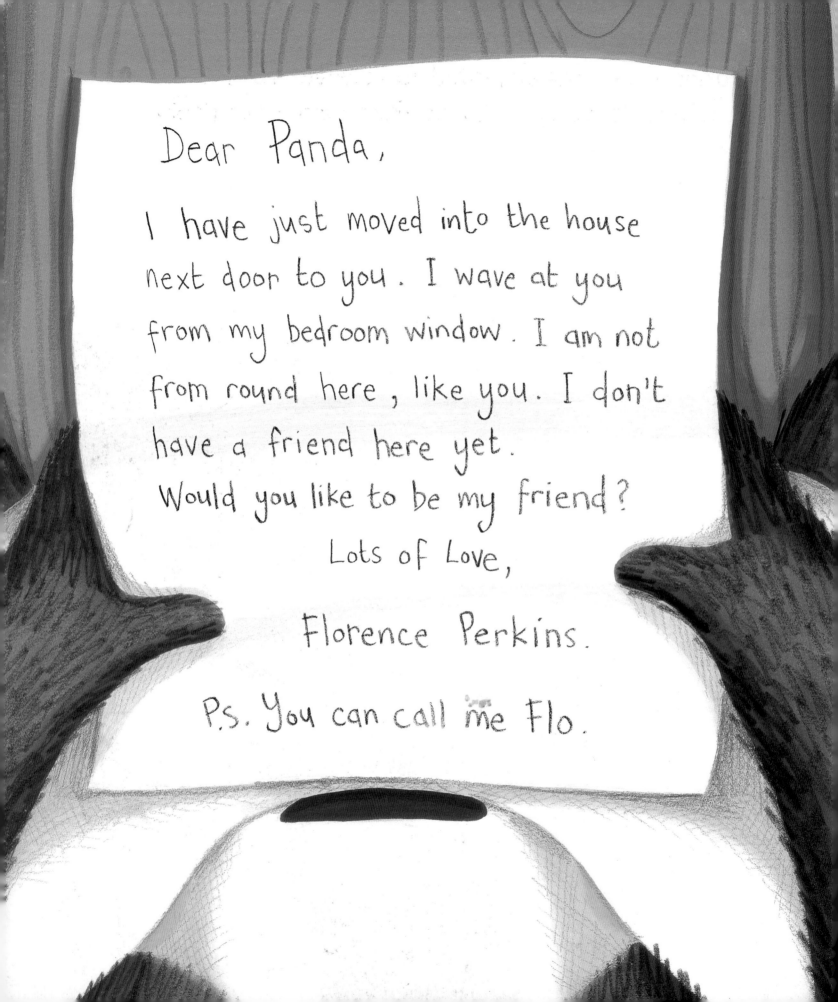

Dear Panda,

I have just moved into the house next door to you. I wave at you from my bedroom window. I am not from round here, like you. I don't have a friend here yet.
Would you like to be my friend?
Lots of Love,

Florence Perkins.

P.s. You can call me Flo.

Panda was flabbergasted to receive his first ever letter. He pondered, and then wrote his reply.

Flo jumped up and down with joy when she received the letter addressed to her in the post.

She tore it open.

So Flo and Panda began
writing back and forth
to each other.

To Panda,
Thank you for the bamboo
pencil. I love it. Here is one of
my pencils for you.
Panda, would you like to come
over to my house to play?
Mum says it's ok.
Bye,
Love Flo.
x

Panda read his second letter.
He grinned, and then wrote
his reply.

Dear Flo,
Yes please,
Love Panda.

So the next day Panda arrived
at Flo's front door.
   "Hello, Panda!" said Flo. "I want to
know all about you. Let's go outside
and play together."

"Can you climb like this, Panda?" said Flo.
   "I'm OK at climbing," called down Panda.

"And can you swim like me, Panda? Can you?" asked Flo.
"A little," called Panda.

"What about hiding – can you hide as well as this?" said Flo.

"Panda? Panda?
Where are you,
Panda?" called Flo.

"What about hula-hooping?"
asked Flo.

"You are funny," she laughed,
looking over at Panda, who
was a little stuck.

"I am so glad that we are friends, Panda," said Flo.

"Yup," grinned Panda.

"But I'm worried about making friends at my new school. What if none of them are as nice as you, and they don't like climbing or swimming or hiding like us?" Flo said.

"Hmmmm," thought Panda, and he whispered
an idea of how he might help.

On Monday morning it was time for Flo to go to school. The classroom was full of chattering children, and even though her new teacher looked very kind, Flo felt very nervous and alone.

She stood in front of the class, and Miss Brook said: "We have a new pupil joining us this year. Meet Florence, class!"

"Hello, Florence!"

the class chorused.

"Florence, can you tell us a little bit about yourself?" said Miss Brook.

"My name is Florence," Flo said quietly, "and my favourite food is toast with jam. I like swimming, climbing, hiding and playing with my hula-hoop, and . . . my best friend is a panda."

The class went quiet. They all stared at Flo. Then they erupted into raucous laughter. "It's true!" Flo nodded. "I've brought him to school to meet you all."

She pointed into the playground and . . .

...sure enough, there was
Panda waving at them all.

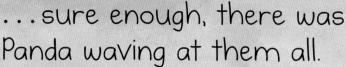

The class squealed with delight.
Miss Brook let them all run outside
to meet him.

Everyone thought Panda was wonderful,
but soon Miss Brook told them they
had to go inside to have their lesson.

As they trailed back in, one girl stayed close to Panda.

"Hullo," smiled Panda.
"Hi, I'm Bea," she gasped.
"Pandas are my favourite!"

"Mine too!" said Flo,
smiling nervously at Bea.

Panda grinned as Flo and Bea excitedly began to talk about pandas to each other.

"Perhaps we can all play together at break time?" said Flo.
"Yes please," beamed Bea, "and you can come and sit next to me in class if you like."

"Oh, yes please," said Flo,
"but what about you, Panda?"
"Time to go home," smiled Panda.
"Oh no!" Flo sniffed. "I don't want you to go."
"Neither do I," said Bea.
"Perhaps you two can come and visit me
soon?" Panda suggested.

"Yes, yes, of course we will," they nodded together.

Panda walked home, happy that he had been able to help his friend Flo find a friend.

Flo and Bea soon found out that they liked a lot of the same things: swimming,

playing hide-and-seek,

hula-hooping,

but most of all they especially liked . . .

. . . PANDAS!